To Ramona Margaret Wheeler Korn
M. B.

To my highly creative dad
I. A.

Text copyright © 2019 by Mac Barnett
Illustrations copyright © 2019 by Isabelle Arsenault

First edition 2019

Library of Congress Catalog Card Number 2019938997
ISBN 978-0-7636-9680-1

19 20 21 22 23 24 APS 10 9 8 7 6 5 4 3 2

Printed in Humen, Dongguan, China

This book was typeset in Bauer Grotesk.
The illustrations were done in gouache, pencil,
and watercolor and assembled digitally.

Candlewick Press
99 Dover Street
Somerville, Massachusetts 02144

visit us at www.candlewick.com

# JUST
## BECAUSE

Mac Barnett

illustrated by

Isabelle Arsenault

CANDLEWICK PRESS

Millions of years ago, thousands of asteroids fell on the earth.

But the dinosaurs
had planned for this.
They fastened themselves
to big balloons,
floated up to space,
and stayed there.

What are black holes?